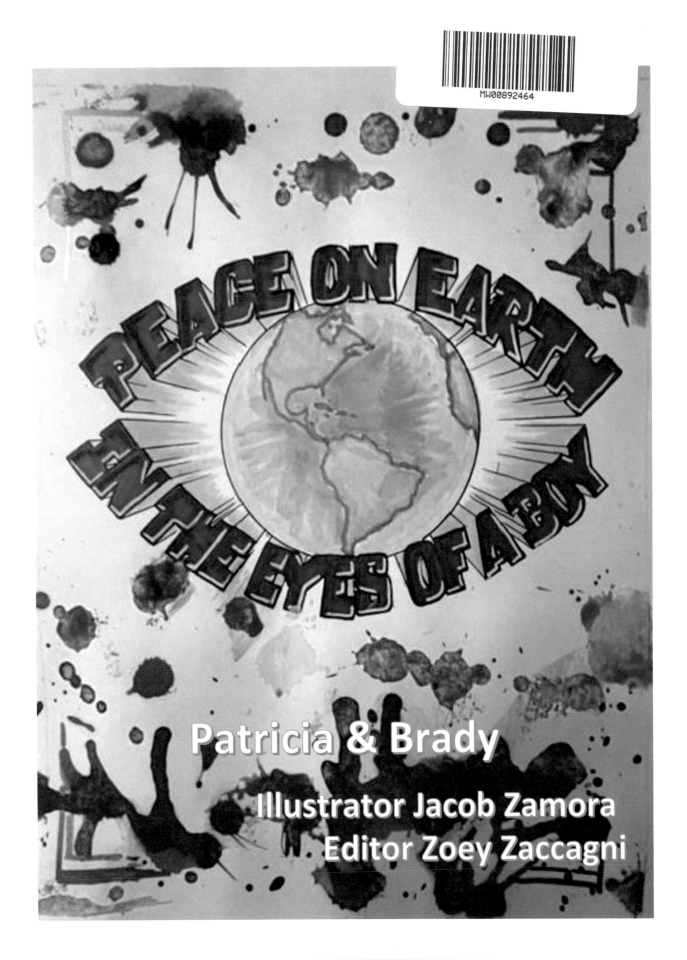

PEACE ON EARTH IN THE EYES OF A BOY

Patricia & Brady

Illustrator Jacob Zamora
Editor Zoey Zaccagni

Dedication

To our family and friends, who are making this world a better place .

Trish

To my monkeys- my kids, nephews, and nieces. My brother Bryan and his family.

This is for you, Love you all.

Jacob

SPECIAL TRAITS AND SUPERHERO GIFTS

Prince Oliver: **Self-Awareness**

Goddess of Treats: **Empathy**

Princess Penelope: **Commitment**

Reddog: **Supportive Companionship**

Cape in Boots: **Supportive Companionship**

Princess Lovebage: **Kindness**

Princess Allwork: **Leadership**

Zen: **Courage**

Aunt Delilah: **Sense of Humor**

Gifts of a Superhero

The Hearts Council grandly strolls into the magnificent hall where legendary Superheroes and observers are sitting in hundreds of rows of chairs, eagerly waiting for the ceremony to begin. The Council consists of retired Superheroes, scientists who protect the planet and animals, and leaders who help people in need. The Hearts Council decides when and why it is right to give a human being Superhero status and bestow upon them special hero gifts.

Today, Prince Oliver accepts his Superhero status and receives his special hero gifts, becoming the youngest Superhero of all time. Young Prince Oliver watches the Council sit in their distinguished seats. Nervously, he looks up at his mother, Princess Penelope, standing beside him fluttering her multicolored fairy wings. She smiles at him warmly and reassures him, "Oliver, you are ready to be a Superhero. You are accountable for your actions, empathetic towards others, and aim for peace on earth." She adds, "Son, look around the room - your entire family and friends are here to support you." Oliver turns his head slightly, to glance upon his Superhero family as they watch the formal procession of the Hearts Council enter the banner- adorned hall. Instantly, he felt an umbrella of calmness and love around him.

He immediately makes eye contact with his grandmother, Goddess of Treats. Oliver loves her dearly and knows he can accomplish anything with her love and support. She proudly winks at the prince and smiles at him lovingly.

Sitting beside her is Oliver's beloved Uncle Reddog. Noticing Oliver's nervousness, Reddog leans forward in his chair towards the prince and whispers words of encouragement, "Nephew, it's okay - we're all here to support you and are enormously proud of you, little man." Oliver smiles slightly and whispers back, "Thank you, Uncle." The Prince quickly scans the hall again and realizes his Aunt Delilah is not there. The absence of his aunt distracts Oliver from the ceremony for a moment.

He quickly refocuses and turns back around to face the Council. His eyes lock with the piercing gaze of Zen, the leader of the Hearts. Zen gruffly asks, "Are you ready, my boy?" Oliver stands up straight and takes a breath then replies calmly, "Yes, sir, I am."

Zen is the man Oliver respects most in the world - not only is he the most revered and courageous Superhero of all time, but he is also Oliver's grandfather.

Zen grandly stands up, and moves towards the podium, to begin the ceremony. He firmly declares to everyone in the hall, "We are all gathered here today to witness Prince Oliver receive his Superhero status and his hero gifts." He then directs his attention to Oliver, "Prince Oliver, this status comes with great responsibility. You will receive a hero call button placed upon your hand to alert all Superheroes. You will have wings upon your back, allowing you to fly at supersonic speed. Upon receiving and accepting these gifts, you will begin training at the Superhero School to learn the responsibility and accountability of your hero gifts. Do you accept your Superhero status and your special gifts?"

Oliver takes a deep breath and replies, "Yes, sir, I accept the Superhero life and all of the responsibilities that comes with this great honor."

The roar of the crowd fills the great hall. The Hearts Council stands in unison and chants, "Believe, Trust, and Help others!" Oliver's family quickly rises to their feet, applauding loudly and shouting together, "Prince Oliver, the youngest of all Superheroes!" A bright light suddenly flutters on Oliver's left hand, and a yellow hero call button magically appears. Just as abruptly, white, gigantic angelic wings materialize on his back.

Zen, in heroic strides, swiftly leaves the podium and proudly wraps his gigantic arms around the boy.

Princess Allwork, Oliver's aunt, walks towards her nephew and lovingly says, "Your cousins look up to you, Oliver. Show them what a great Superhero is, okay?" Oliver's younger cousin excitedly hugs the new Superhero and says, "I am going to be just like you." Princess Allwork smiles at Oliver and swiftly walks away with the young child close behind. Immediately, Reddog, Princess Lovebage and Cape in Boots fly over with the help of their jet-powered boots. The Princess kindly says, "We're always here for you. If you ever need anything, call us." Oliver grins at her and feels overjoyed by all the love shown towards him.

He hugs his uncle and aunt goodbye and pets Cape in Boots.

Oliver walks towards the majestic hall's exit door and becomes distracted again. "Where is Aunt Delilah? She would never miss a chance to see the family and my Superhero ceremony," he pondered.

Unaware of the Darkness

Lost in thought, after his first day at Superhero School Prince Oliver trudges towards his grandparents' house, unaware of the impending darkness. He doesn't notice the murky puddles left behind from the spring thunderstorm. As he walks, his untied shoelaces drag through the water collecting dirt and grime from the sidewalk.

Oliver is torn between the importance of his Superhero schooling and why his Aunt Delilah is still missing. Oliver works to regulate his emotions as frustration wells up inside him.

Approaching his grandparents' house, Oliver notices the unusual state of the neighbors' yards. The grass is black and sludgy like a million earthworms. "That's weird. I've never seen grass look like that," he contemplated. He glances up at the sky and looming above him, he spots a gigantic menacing cloud growing darker and more powerful by the second. It is unlike any cloud he has ever seen.

More aware of the gloomy developments around him, Oliver hastens his pace.

Oliver runs into his grandparents' house. He tries to catch his breath and swiftly wraps his arms around Goddess of Treats. She grabs him with her outstretched hands. She quickly realizes the young prince is shaking with fear and hugs him more tightly than usual. She asks him with compassion and empathy in her voice, "Oliver, what is wrong? You're shaking so much you're going to come right out of your shoes."

Breathlessly, the Prince whimpers, "Grandma, something terrible is happening outside! All the grass is turning black, and a scary dark cloud is taking over the sky!"

With a worried expression but a stillness in her voice Goddess of Treats says, "Oh dear, Oliver, you need to listen." Knowing the Prince is frightened, she calmly continues, "It's time to use the valuable knowledge you're learning at Superhero School. Please, push your hero call button. We need the other Superheroes to find Aunt Delilah. I believe she is the key to all the darkness taking over the world."

Oliver quizzically glances at his grandma and promptly pushes his hero call button.

The Spreading Darkness

Across town, not too long after Reddog, Princess Lovebage, and Cape in Boots start an intense fetch - frisbee game with the other dogs at the park, the sky is quickly engulfed by a menacing cloud. Cape in Boots, suddenly starts barking ferociously up at the powerful approaching darkness and the Princess notices the grass is now black and squishy. The Superheroes call buttons begin to rapidly flash.

Reddog consoles Cape in Boots and firmly states, "My mighty crusader, Prince Oliver is calling us. We must fly to our young hero." Obediently, the four-legged hero stops barking and runs to the side of his protector. Rapidly, Princess Lovebage snaps her Superhero pearl bracelet into multiple dog leashes to guide the other loose dogs in the park back to their homes.

Concerned, Reddog ignites his red jet-powered boots alongside Cape in Boots and turns to wave goodbye to the Princess. She waves back towards the flying duo and calls out, "I'll meet up with you guys as soon as I know these dogs are safe!"

Down the street, from the three crusaders, Princess Penelope hastily finishes her work as her hero call button speedily starts flashing. She rushes outside to see the most horrendous, billowing black cloud. She immediately flutters her multicolored fairy wings as she speeds into the sky; she fumbles frantically into her jean pockets to make sure she has her Superhero ALL-FIX-IT tool. Not concentrating, she accidentally nose-dives into a larger-than-life slimy, dead tree. Spotting the imminent disaster, Reddog swiftly swoops down and grabs the back of her shirt as Cape in Boots yanks her shoe to prevent her from hitting her head.

"Hey, sis! What are you doing diving headfirst? You know how to fly!" Reddog jokingly giggles as Princess Penelope recovers her upright flight. She gives him a half-smile and worriedly says, "Prince Oliver needs us." Reddog assures her, "I know, sis, we're all on our way. Princess Lovebage is not far behind. She is taking a few dogs to safety."

Cape in Boots barks in agreement and leads the two sibling heroes through the dismal sky.

Many miles away from her family, Princess Allwork lovingly gathers her three children. Using her Superhero gift of pausing time, she proceeds to get them ready for the day. The three little ones begin to bounce out the door one by one in pursuit of imaginary creatures. She happily follows, then stops abruptly behind her ever so still children staring at the sky. A mysterious cloud seems to be consuming the roof of her house and her lawn resembles an oil spill.

She instantly glances down at her hand where her hero call button is persistently blinking. Without hesitation, she picks up all three children, carries them to her flying car, and carefully buckles them into their car seats. The two oldest boys in unison ask, "Why is the sky eating at our house and why is the grass slippery and gross?" In a caring, but calm voice, as she jumps into the car, she explains, "We are going on an unexpected adventure. Prince Oliver needs us. and I believe it's because of the cloud eating at our house and why our grass is disgusting."

She grabs the steering wheel and flies at supersonic speed towards Oliver's Superhero call, while her three children look in awe towards the menacing darkness.

Peace on Earth

It has only been a few minutes since Oliver pressed his hero button. He suddenly hears feet scampering on the porch and Princess Allwork's flying mobile speed to a halt in front of the house. He swings open the door to see his Superhero family standing on the porch. Oliver excitedly runs towards them and instantly grabs Princess Penelope's hand. Oliver leads the family quickly towards the Hero Work Room.

Addressing Goddess of Treats, Reddog begins," Mom, what is going on?" While looking around the hero table, Goddess of Treats grimly says, "I'm afraid Aunt Delilah's disappearance is the cause of all this darkness." Her gaze stops at Prince Oliver and firmly continues, "We all have learned at Superhero School if we lose our individual traits our world will no longer have peace and will become dark. Since all of us have our traits, I believe Aunt Delilah has lost hers." Princess Lovebage agrees, "You're right. The world is black and unpeaceful since Aunt Delilah disappeared." The Superheroes all nod in agreement. Princess Allwork adds in her leadership voice, "We need to split up and search all over the world for her."

All the Superheroes in agreement reply together, "Believe, Trust, and Help others!" They all speedily leave in their separate directions while Goddess of Treats stays behind to look over the small children.

A few minutes later, Prince Oliver and Princess Penelope are standing outside a small dark building. Oliver peers through the window to see his Aunt Delilah hunched over, looking sad. Oliver once again presses his hero call button. Just as Princess Penelope pulls out her ALL-FIX-IT tool to open the building door, the other Superheroes arrive from all over the world.

Oliver points through the window while he explains, "There is Aunt Delilah. But look, there is a mean-looking dog guarding the door." Princess Allwork hastily suggests, "Princess Penelope, you open the door with your ALL-FIX-IT tool. Reddog, Princess Lovebage and Cape in Boots subdue the dog. I will stop time so Prince Oliver can guide Aunt Delilah out the door." They all agree and softly chant "Believe, Trust, and Help others."

In a split-second, Princess Allwork halts human time while Princess Penelope opens the door; Princess Lovebage secures the aggressive dog with her multi-leash; Reddog subdues the canine with a gentle touch on his head; Cape in Boots puts his trusted hat around the growling dog's mouth; and Oliver briskly walks Aunt Delilah out of the building.

In a daze, Aunt Delilah looks around at her family. She faintly asks, "What is going on?" Oliver gently hugs her and says, "You lost your special trait of laughter, and the world became dark." Aunt Delilah affectionately looks at her nephew and shyly explains, "I was so sad and lonely because I felt unneeded. All of you have the greatest hero gifts and traits; mine do not compare. I thought no one would miss me." Princess Penelope chimed in, "The world is only beautiful and peaceful if we ALL use our individual traits and special gifts."

Looking at Aunt Delilah, Reddog adds, "For the world to have peace we need your Sense of Humor, Prince Oliver's Self-Awareness, Princess Penelope's Commitment, Goddess of Treats' Empathy, Zen's Courage, Princess Lovebage's Kindness, Princess Allwork's Leadership, and mine and Cape in Boots Supportive Companionship."

Princess Allwork looks at Oliver and adds, "Remember, what we learned at Superhero School, we all need to rely on each other and use our unique traits and special gifts for world peace to exist."

The superhero family chants, "Believe, Trust, and Help others!"

This is Peace in the Eyes of a Boy.

In Memory, Our Heroes

Georgia Gutierrez and Linda Williams

Connie, Grandma Deloras, Aunt Holly, and brother Ed Hun

About Illustrator

This is my first rodeo illustrating a book. I started drawing at eight years old. Then at twenty three I began airbrushing that led me to a tattoo apprenticeship at twenty six. I eventually ventured off on my own as a tattoo artist. To become the illustrator for the children book series "In the Eyes of a Boy" is a dream come true. I am extremely grateful for all the people in my life that have always shown support for my art.

Jacob Zamora

Made in the USA
Thornton, CO
10/24/24 17:34:26

72503f7c-807e-42e9-8159-b953bbb5bbe7R01